HE____ O____ ____!

I'm _____ er.

As I'm sure you know from my brother's bestselling novels, I'm a special correspondent for *The Rodent's Gazette*, Mouse Island's most famouse newspaper. Unlike my 'fraidy mouse brother, I absolutely adore traveling, having adventures, and meeting rodents from all around the world!

The adventure I want to tell you about begins at Mouseford Academy, the school I went to when I was a young mouseling. I had such a great experience there as a student that I came back to teach a journalism class.

When I returned as a grown mouse, I met five really special students: Colette, Nicky, Pamela, Paulina, and Violet. You could hardly imagine five more different mouselings, but they became great friends right away. And they liked me so much that they decided to name their group after me: the Thea Sisters! I was so touched by that, I decided to write about their adventures. So turn the page to read a fabumouse adventure about the

THEA SiSTERS!

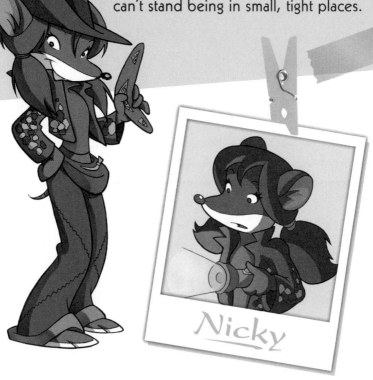

Name: Nicky

Nickname: Nic

Home: Australia

Secret ambition: Wants to be an ecologist.

Loves: Open spaces and nature.

Strengths: She is always in a good mood, as long as she's outdoors!

Weaknesses: She can't sit still!

Secret: Nicky is claustrophobic—she can't stand being in small, tight places.

nicky

Nicky

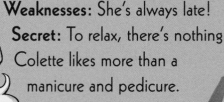

COLETTE

Name: Colette

Nickname: It's Colette, please. (She can't stand nicknames.)

Home: France

Secret ambition: Colette is very particular about her appearance. She wants to be a fashion writer.

Loves: The color pink.

Strengths: She's energetic and full of great ideas.

Weaknesses: She's always late!

Secret: To relax, there's nothing Colette likes more than a manicure and pedicure.

Colette

Name: Violet
Nickname: Vi
Home: China

Secret ambition: Wants to become a great violinist.
Loves: Books! She is a real intellectual, just like my brother, Geronimo.
Strengths: She's detail-oriented and always open to new things.
Weaknesses: She is a bit sensitive and can't stand being teased. And if she doesn't get enough sleep, she can be a real grouch!
Secret: She likes to unwind by listening to classical music and drinking green tea.

VIOLET

Violet

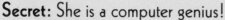

Name: Paulina
Nickname: Polly
Home: Peru
Secret ambition: Wants to be a scientist.
Loves: Traveling and meeting people from all over the world. She is also very close to her sister, Maria.
Strengths: Loves helping other rodents.
Weaknesses: She's shy and can be a bit clumsy.
Secret: She is a computer genius!

PAULINA

PAULINA

Name: Pamela
Nickname: Pam
Home: Tanzania
Secret ambition: Wants to become a sports journalist or a car mechanic.
Loves: Pizza, pizza, and more pizza! She'd eat pizza for breakfast if she could.
Strengths: She is a peacemaker. She can't stand arguments.
Weaknesses: She is very impulsive.
Secret: Give her a screwdriver and any mechanical problem will be solved!

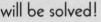

PAMELA

Pamela

Geronimo Stilton

Thea Stilton
AND THE DANCING SHADOWS

Scholastic Inc.

ISBN 978-0-545-48187-8

Text by Thea Stilton
Original title *Mistero dietro le quinte*
Cover by Arianna Rea (pencils), Yoko Ippolitoni (inks), and Ketty Formaggio (color)
Illustrations by Sabrina Ariganello, Michela Frare, Daniela Geremia, Cristina Giorgilli, Sonia Matrone, Gaetano Petrigno, Roberta Pierpaoli, Arianna Rea, and Roberta Tedeschi
Color by Cinzia Antonielli, Alessandra Bracaglia, Edwin Nori, and Elena Sanjust
Graphics by Paola Cantoni with Marta Lorini

Special thanks to Beth Dunfey
Translated by Emily Clement
Interior design by Kay Petronio

12 11 10 9 8 7 6 5 4 3 2 1   13 14 15 16 17 18/0

Printed in the U.S.A.   40
First printing, March 2013

A SPECIAL APPOINTMENT

It was a cool spring evening in New Mouse City, and the hall at the **Rabid Rodent Readers' Club** was slowly emptying out. I had just finished reading from my latest book.

Wavering whiskers, how I love meeting my readers in the fur! Oh, pardon me, I nearly forgot to introduce myself. My name is **THEA STILTON**, and I'm a special correspondent for *The Rodent's Gazette*. I travel all around the world, chasing stories. Between adventures, what I love more than anything is writing!

"Thea, your new **book** is fabumouse!" cried Lucy,

the readers' club president. "Why don't we celebrate with dinner at Le Squeakery? They have some **MARVEMOUSE** cheeses."

The invitation was tempting, but I had to decline. "Thank you so much, but tonight I have a SPECIAL appointment — with my TV set! My students, the Thea Sisters, are going to appear on cable."

A little while back, I'd been invited to teach a class in adventure journalism

at my old school, Mouseford Academy. Colette, nicky, PAMELA, PAULINA, and **Violet** — the Thea Sisters — were in my class. Without a doubt, they are the five brainiest, most talented mouselets I've ever met.

Tonight, a cable channel dedicated to ballet was showing a special program direct from **LA SCALA** theater in Milan, Italy — one of the most **FAMOUSE** theaters in the world. The **THEA SISTERS** would be performing onstage! That morning, I had received a **text** from Paulina telling me when to tune in. I couldn't wait to see the mouselets dancing their tails off!

But to tell you how this latest **adventure** began, I need to rewind a few months, to a rainy afternoon on **WHALE ISLAND**. . . .

BRAVO, MOUSELETS!

Professor Plié's squeaks of encouragement echoed against the **mirrored** walls of Mouseford Academy's DANCE studio. "Bravo, Violet! Move that paw a little higher — that's it!"

The students were in the middle of freestyle, everyone's favorite part of ballet class. This was always **Violet's** time to shine.

"Violet is more graceful than a gliding swan!" Colette whispered admiringly as she **WATCHED** her friend twirl.

"This classical DANCE class is just perfect for her," Pam agreed. "I, on the other paw, have all the agility of a **MONSTER TRUCK**."

Nicky gave her an affectionate pat on the

tail. "Oh, please, no can one touch you when it comes to step dancing!"

Just then, the bell rang to end class. BBBBRRRIIIIIINNNGGGG!

The students reluctantly headed to the LOCKER ROOM. Professor Plié's dance class was very POPULAR, and it always seemed to end too early.

"Why the LONG snouts?" Professor Plié called out. "Your other classes are waiting!"

Then she moved closer to the Thea Sisters. "And Professor Ratyshnikov is waiting for the five of you," she continued quietly. "Please report directly to her office!"

The mouselets exchanged a surprised look: The director of the performing arts department had never asked them to a group meeting before! They SCURRIED to her office as FAST as their paws could carry them.

"**MOUSELETS**, do you think it's about rehearsal?" Colette asked anxiously. "I know I *missed* a lot of beats. . . ."

"No way!" Nicky dismissed that idea. "You were great!"

"I hope it's not about my final paper on CELTIC music. Maybe it wasn't long enough. . . ." Paulina said.

"It could be about any of us," said Violet, **PERPLEXED**. "But why have us all come in a group?"

Pam **cut** her off. "Let's go in and see!"

So, with tails trembling, the five FRIENDS entered Professor Ratyshnikov's office.

A DANCE OF DISTRESS!

Professor Ratyshnikov raised her eyes from her laptop and smiled. "Ah, here you are! I've called you here because I need your **HELP**." The professor stood up and started to **PACE** back and forth like a cat outside a mouse hole. "I'm sure you know that the dance world is very tOUGH. Competition among dancers is fiercer than a fight between sewer rats. But with sacrifice and **passion**, the most talented students make careers for themselves on the professional stage."

The mouselets nodded and continued listening.

"Shortcuts and tricks never work!" the professor went on. "At least, they never have before now. . . ."

She shook her snout. "You see, I'm afraid someone is trying to **fix** the world's most important international ballet competition."

Colette **GASPED**. "What? That's impossible!"

Professor Ratyshnikov gave the hint of a **SMILE**. "I knew you'd react the same way I did. That's why I've gathered you here." She approached the **LARGE** screen on her office wall. "I'll leave the explanation to my old friend and colleague, Madame Rattlova."

Violet couldn't believe her ears. "You mean the **famouse** Madame Natalya Rattlova?!"

The professor nodded as she **fiddled** with a remote control.

Violet noticed her friends' **CURIOUS LOOKS**. It was obvious they didn't have a clue who Madame Rattlova was. "We're going to be squeaking with a true STAR," she explained. "Madame Rattlova is one of the most important Russian **ballerinas** in history! Now she runs a highly **respected** ballet school in Moscow."

A light squeak interrupted them. "Thank you for the kind introduction, my dear!"

The mouselets **TURNED** toward the screen: A rodent with a **SWEET** smile and a proud eXPResSion had appeared. It was Madame Rattlova.

The **GREAT** ballerina told the mouselets that the dance world was in big **trouble**.

About a year ago, a ᴺᵉʷ agency had appeared on the ballet scene. Within a few months, they had placed a large number of ᵞᴼᵁᴺᴳ, unknown dancers under contract.

"The agency is called 𝓜ice 𝓯or 𝓓ance," Madame Rattlova explained. "Their dancers have won 𝖺𝗅𝗅 the ballet competitions this year . . . even when they didn't deserve to!"

"Lately I've been hearing a lot of **NEGATIVE** comments about Mice for Dance," Professor Ratyshnikov added. "Several of my colleagues have been upset by the ⅠⓃⒸⓇⒺⒹⒾⒷⓁⒺ number of times their dancers have won competitions. Especially because many of their performances haven't been up to par."

"The agency has also been sending their

dancers to ทі̃gิhtсlบ‍ฮ openings, gala evenings, and movie premieres," Madame Rattlova continued. "The agency is paid large sums of money for their appearances. But the dancers are so busy appearing in public that they don't have time to practice. Needless to say, the quality of their performances has suffered GREATLY!"

"The agency isn't in this business out of love for dance," Professor Ratyshnikov concluded. "They're just doing it to make a quick buck!"

The agency Mice for Dance has monopolized amateur dance competitions. But their main motivation isn't love of dance ... it's money!

STOLEN DREAMS

The mouselets were **stunned** into squeaklessness.

"But if the dancers from 𝑀𝑖𝑐𝑒 𝑓𝑜𝑟 𝐷𝑎𝑛𝑐𝑒 aren't up to snuff, how do they win so many competitions?" Nicky asked at last.

Paulina nodded. "The judges at these international competitions are all **ARTISTS** of the **highest** level, right? Why would they compromise their ethics?"

Madame Rattlova sighed. "Unfortunately, Mice for Dance was created by expert choreographers and artistic directors. We're afraid that, thanks to their experience and reputations, they've gained support from some of the most respected figures in the DANCE world."

Professor Ratyshnikov stepped in to explain. "We suspect that the agency has used **cash** bribes to **CORRUPT** choreographers and directors at the biggest ballet companies. That's how they've **INFILTRATED** the judging panels and fixed the competitions!"

The Thea Sisters mumbled **INDIGNANTLY**.

"Participating in a competition is a **dream** for many young dancers," Pam sputtered.

LA SCALA — MILAN, ITALY

The La Scala opera house opened in 1778. It was named for the church Santa Maria della Scala, which once stood on the same spot. La Scala became known for showcasing Italian opera and was home to the great conductor Toscanini. It also houses a famous dance company, the **La Scala Theatre Ballet**.

BOLSHOI THEATRE — MOSCOW, RUSSIA

Built in 1825, the Bolshoi is one of the most famous theaters in the world for opera and ballet. In Russian, its name (also written as *Bol'šoj*) means "great." The **Bolshoi Ballet** is known for their amazing productions of classic and children's ballets. Dancers trained at the Bolshoi School are among the best in the world.

There are many theaters in the world that are home to prestigious ballet companies. Here are a few of the most famous.

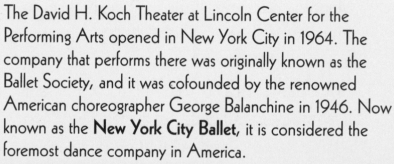

LINCOLN CENTER — NEW YORK, U.S.A.

The David H. Koch Theater at Lincoln Center for the Performing Arts opened in New York City in 1964. The company that performs there was originally known as the Ballet Society, and it was cofounded by the renowned American choreographer George Balanchine in 1946. Now known as the **New York City Ballet**, it is considered the foremost dance company in America.

ROYAL OPERA HOUSE — LONDON, ENGLAND

The Royal Opera House is also known by the name Covent Garden, after the square in London where it's located. The original building was constructed in 1732. Since then, it has been demolished and rebuilt many times. After a fire in 1856, it reopened in its current form in 1858. Today the opera house is home to the most important ballet company in the United Kingdom, the **Royal Ballet**.

"A dream that takes time, **HARD** work, and lots of rehearsal to fulfill!"

Violet agreed. "We've got to stop those cheats!"

Madame Rattlova smiled. "You mouselets sound like you have the *energy* we need to uncover this scam!"

"Mouselets, this is our plan," Professor Ratyshnikov continued. "In just a few days, Madame Rattlova's school will present several of its students at the international competition at **LA SCALA** in Milan, Italy. The rodents in charge of the competition are in the **DARK** about what's going on with the agency," the professor explained. "But we've heard that there are a few judges on the jury who are **WORKING** with Mice for Dance. It's the perfect opportunity to investigate."

"And you will all participate in the contest

so you can interact with the competitors and **investigate** behind the scenes," Madame Rattlova explained.

"You must leave *immediately* for Milan," Professor Ratyshnikov declared, pawing the mouselets five plane tickets. "You have seats on the next **FLIGHT**!"

AS DIFFERENT AS PARMESAN AND PROVOLONE

The **THEA SiSTERS** barely had time to pack their *bags* before they left for Italy. As soon as their flight landed in Milan, the mouselets hopped in a **TAXI** to their hotel.

A golden **sunset** sparkled brightly on the windows and the **WATER** of the Navigli canals. It was the perfect greeting for the five friends after their long journey.

Violet was excited. "Mouselets, my tail is already **twitching** with trepidation! How in the name of **CHEESE** can we compete with dancers who have been training for years?"

"Uh-oh, if *you're* **worried**, then we're all in big trouble! You're the **BEST** dancer

MILAN

Milan is located in northern Italy. It is one of Italy's most modern cities, and is the country's financial and commercial center. Today it is considered one of the world's international capitals of fashion and design, along with Paris, London, and New York.

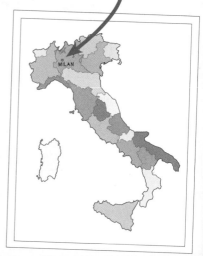

we've got," Pam reminded her. "What about me? I've got two left paws!"

Paulina laughed. "Don't worry, Pam!" she **reassured** her friend. "I've been reading up on the rules. The competitors who don't make it to the finals can still participate in the *gala performance*."

Nicky nodded. "That'll definitely make it easier for us to investigate the agency's **tricks**. Remember, that's why we're here!"

"Just think of the **GORGEOUS** costumes we'll get to wear to the gala!" Colette said, clapping her paws. The French mouselet had a **passion** for fashion.

Soon they pulled up to their hotel. The lobby was **packed** with mouselets and ratlings from all over the world chattering in many different languages.

"**SMOKIN' SWISS CHEESE!**" exclaimed

Pam. "What an international atmosphere! Hey, look over there. It's Madame Rattlova!"

Madame Rattlova was *hurrying* over. With her were two ratlings of about the same age and height as each other. One had **DARK** hair and seemed lost in his own thoughts. The other was *blond* and walked with his snout held high. He was gazing at the mouselets **CURIOUSLY**.

"**Welcome!**" the former ballerina greeted them. "May I present my two best students, Pyotr and Vasily. They're cousins, although they're so **DIFFERENT** that sometimes I think they came from two different **PLANETS**!" She winked. "Oh, and they also happen to be my nephews."

Vasily, the blond ratling, bowed gracefully. "**Pleased** to meet you," he said cheerfully. He looked around the group, letting his eyes

rest on Violet for a moment.

Pyotr greeted the mouselets in a calm, **DEEP** voice. "Thank you for your help. When this is all over, you must be our guests in Russia."

"Now come along, ratlings," their aunt said. "Don't **distract** our new friends with your chatter!"

Pyotr was a little more discreet than his cousin, but while Madame Rattlova was squeaking, he **SHOT** a glance at Violet.

This *move* didn't escape Colette's expert eye. She loved playing matchmouser. She SMILED, thinking it might be fun to watch these two handsome young ratlings compete for her shy friend's attention.

"They're as different as Parmesan and **provolone**," she said to herself. "But which one would be better for our dear Vi?"

WHAT A BULLY!

Madame Rattlova offered to turn in the Thea Sisters' **OFFICIAL** registration paperwork at the front desk.

"I'm going to sign in the mouselets," she told her nephews. "You two try to stay out of **trouble** for a few minutes, okay?"

"Yes, Sarge . . . I mean, Aunt Natalya!" Vasily snapped to attention with a **smirk**, making the mouselets **giggle**.

Pyotr didn't seem to hear what his aunt had said. He turned to **Violet**. "Let me give you a paw with your luggage. I didn't catch your name. . . ."

Violet introduced herself and smiled. "It's a pleasure to meet you."

At that moment, the glass doors of the

hotel opened, and five new dancers strode in.

"Those are the dancers from *Mice for Dance*," Pyotr murmured.

The two mouselets and three ratlings traveled in a tight group. They had a *snooty* look about them. All the other dancers moved aside as they scampered by. Paulina noticed

that many of the mice in the lobby seemed *intimidated*.

But that didn't stop the crowd from LAUGHING when the tall, muscular dancer leading the group tripped over a stray gym bag.

"**HEY!**" he shouted. He stumbled and staggered for a few steps. The two mouselets from Mice for Dance quickly came to his aid, while the other two ratlings **LOOKED** around threateningly.

"Whose bag is this?!" **yelled** one of the ratlings.

"Ex-excuse me . . ." a small voice replied. "It's mine. . . ."

A slender mouselet approached them **FEARFULLY**. She had beautiful brown eyes and **THICK** blonde fur held back in a braid.

The **CLUMSY** dancer shook his paw at her. "Don't you know **WHO** I am?! I'm Gaspard Roditeur!" he barked. "You could have **destroyed** the career of the greatest *étoile** of the Paris Opera, furface!"

The lobby was so quiet, you could hear a cheese slice drop. Everyone **STARED** at the **BULLY** and the poor mouselet who'd accidentally sparked his anger.

The Mice for Dance troupe behaves so arrogantly, and Gaspard Roditeur is particularly confident! Why is he so certain that he'll become a star?

Étoile means "star" in French. The term usually refers to the lead dancer in a ballet company.

LiKE A FAiRY TALE!

The Thea Sisters and their new friends were **shaking** with outrage: It wasn't right to treat someone that way!

Pyotr **leaped** forward. "Leave her alone! She didn't do anything **wrong**," he told Gaspard. The Thea Sisters followed, standing between the mouselet and her accusers.

Gaspard shot them an **icy** look. "Who are you, her bodyguards?!"

"We don't like **BULLIES**," Vasily replied, joining his cousin.

Pam quickly intervened: It was turning **ugly**! "Relax, ratlings!" she said. "Let's remember we're all here for the competition."

"**Right!**" Roditeur agreed disdainfully. "We'll work this out **ONSTAGE**."

"You'll wish you could DANCE like us!" one of his companions jeered.

With that, the Mice for Dance group WALKED AWAY, cackling.

The young dancer let out a sigh of relief. "Thank you so much! My name is Carlotta, and I live here in Milan. I just came to confirm my registration. I didn't mean to cause any TROUBLE."

Nicky shook her paw. "I'm *Nicky*. Don't feel bad — you didn't do anything wrong!"

The Thea Sisters *chatted* with Carlotta for a bit. "My mother is the **COSTUME** mistress for La Scala," she told them. "Ever since I was a young mouseling, I've been in *love* with ballet. My *dream* was to enroll in a dance school, but my **family** couldn't afford it. So I practiced on my own."

Carlotta had spent years backstage, studying the **movements** of the greatest ballerinas, hoping to one day dance on the same stage as her heroes.

"This year, I sent my **video** to the selection committee. I could hardly believe it when they called me in!" she concluded, her eyes **shining**. "It's like a fairy tale!"

Carlotta and the THEA SISTERS decided

to meet up the next day at the **official** drawing to determine the **order** of auditions.

Carlotta shot her new friends a SMILE. "Why don't you come a little early? I have a **surprise** for you, to thank you for your help!"

SUSPECTS AND SCHEMES

The next morning, Paulina led the mouselets out of the hotel. She had consulted her trusty **guidebook** to find her way to La Scala.

As soon as they reached the Piazza della Scala, there was no mistaking the *majestic* theater rising into the blue sky!

Carlotta **waved** at them from the main entrance. "Mouselets! Over here!"

After they all said hello, Carlotta revealed her surprise. "Guess what? I got permission to take you on a **behind-the-scenes** tour before the drawing begins!"

She ushered the Thea Sisters through the grand entrance to La Scala. The mouselets were ENCHANTED by the gorgeous marble and gilded walls of the entrance.

The great hall was even more spectacular. "OOOOOOOH!" Colette sighed. "How beautiful! It's like a real palace!"

But the tour was just beginning. "COME ON!" their new friend urged them. "Let me bring you backstage!"

Pam, the group's resident **mechanic**, was astonished by everything hidden in the wings. There were amazing contraptions hanging in midair — RoPeS, electric winches, ladders, and backdrops, all in a complex **maze** of elevated balconies.

"What a sight!" she exclaimed.

Carlotta led the THEA SiSTERS into the rehearsal rooms, the dressing rooms, the chorus rooms, and the orchestra pit.

Their **TOUR** ended on a **LONG** balcony the crew used to manipulate the scenery and backdrops. Over a hundred feet

LA SCALA

La Scala can hold about two thousand spectators, with seats in the orchestra, the mezzanine, and the balconies. The stage itself is enormous — one of the largest in Italy. Behind the curtain, the scenery and the lights are controlled from a large, modern addition to the theater. The theater was restored and expanded in an important renovation that took place between 2002 and 2004.

below them, in the darkness behind the closed curtain, was the stage.

"It's time to go back," Carlotta said. "The judges must be ready by now."

It was impossible to see anything on the **dark** stage, but the mouselets heard some muffled squeaking.

"So," a screechy voice echoed, "I think . . . the card to pick . . ."

"Okay . . . then substitute it with our contestant," another voice replied.

A third squeak, **DEEPER** than the others, joined the first two. "Our dancers . . . must perform first . . . send them quickly . . . PHOTOGRAPHERS . . . fashion magazine . . ."

"What's going on?" Carlotta murmured. "What are they talking about?"

The THEA SISTERS exchanged a nervous look. It was clear to them that the rodents onstage were **plotting** something about the drawing for the competition. What if these were the judges working with *Mice for Dance*?

Just then, the three rodents were interrupted by someone calling out, "Well, my dear colleagues! Shall we begin?"

"I know that squeak!" Carlotta said without

hesitation. "That's Enrico Mousetti, the artistic director of La Scala, I'm sure of it. He's the head judge for the competition."

The conspirators immediately fell silent and followed Signor Mousetti.

"We've got to figure out whose squeaks those were!" Pam muttered.

Something suspicious was going on. But the investigation would have to wait — the selection was about to start, and the mouselets needed to get to the front of the theater!

Who were the three mice plotting in the shadows? What were they talking about?

I OBJECT!

The Thea Sisters and Carlotta **BREATHLESSLY** scurried down to the large, illuminated hall below. The red seats were gradually filling up with **nervous** dancers and teachers, all of whom were waiting to hear the order of the performances.

Pyotr, Vasily, and Madame Rattlova were already there. As soon as they saw the mouselets, they called them over.

"Ah, you're here at last!" Madame Rattlova greeted the mouselets. Then she turned to Carlotta and said *kindly*, "You must be the Italian dancer. These two rascals told me about your troubles yesterday."

Vasily and Pyotr BLUSHED and sneaked a look at the mouselets.

"Um, we may have exaggerated a little bit. . . ." Vasily said sheepishly.

"Unfortunately, this is not the first time the performers from Mice for Dance have behaved so ARROGANTLY," Madame Rattlova said, glancing at the five dancers who had been such BULLIES.

Just then, the heavy scarlet curtain rose, and an expectant silence fell over the hall.

The judges strode onstage and quickly made themselves COMFORTABLE.

"The one with the cane is Signor Mousetti, PRESIDENT of the jury. He's a real CELEBRITY here at La Scala," Carlotta whispered to her FRIENDS, pointing to a distinguished-looking gentlemouse. "They say he's a very strict choreographer."

Madame Rattlova nodded. "He is a brilliant mouse, but his ideas are a little narrow. Mousetti thinks you can only be a great dancer if you attend a **prestigious** school."

Nicky saw Carlotta lower her eyes, and she put a paw on her shoulder to encourage her. "Don't worry, you'll show him how wrong he is!"

"Who are the others?" Pam asked, peering at the members of the jury.

"They're former *dancers*, like me," answered Madame Rattlova, **LOOKING** at the other six judges.

Then she added, in a low squeak, "If there's some **deception** going on, then Mice for Dance must have at least one of these judges in their pocket!"

Signor Mousetti called the hall to order, **frowning** as he consulted his watch. "Well, ladies and gentlemice, let's begin. It's already late, and we mustn't waste any more time."

Madame Mousekaya, a slender but severe-looking rodent, began the drawing for the participants. The first card was passed to Frau Fledermaus, a mouse with **short fur** and dark eyes.

"Gaspard Roditeur!" she announced. "Student of Madame De Bois's **RENOWNED** school in Paris, and a member of Mice for Dance.

Martha Fledermaus

He will be performing a *SOLO* dance."

The THEA SISTERS were startled. The first name drawn was indeed from Mice for Dance. So the three unknown rodents plotting backstage *were* members of the jury!

That was the first of several unpleasant **surprises**. Just as the Thea Sisters had feared, the first five spots were assigned to the performers from Mice for Dance. It was clear that the rodents that they had heard plotting had *sabotaged* the drawing!

The drawing of the *dancers'* names continued without a hitch . . . at least, until it came time to pick the last dancer. That's when Carlotta's name was pulled!

"Carlotta Ratignani!" Frau Fledermaus called out. "Self-taught, registered for the competition as a solo dancer."

The five dancers from Mice for Dance were drawn first. It looks like this is what the three judges were plotting backstage!

The Thea Sisters WHiSPeReD their congratulations to their friend, who looked like she couldn't believe her ears. But a protest from the stage quickly chilled their enthusiasm.

"Self-taught?!?"

That was the squeak of Enrico Mousetti, the president of the jury!

Signor Mousetti SCOWLED at Carlotta. "It's unheard of! Only students from the best schools can participate. We cannot admit her to the competition. I OBJECT!"

Enrico Mousetti

A TRUE BALLERINA

The Thea Sisters were SQUEAKLESS. So was everyone else in the audience.

Nicky was the first to **react**. "I can't believe they'd exclude a dancer just because she hasn't attended a *fancy* dance school. That's crazier than a cat chasing its own tail!"

"Is it possible that Signor Mousetti is working with Mice for Dance?" Pam whispered. "Maybe he's afraid Carlotta is more talented than the dancers from the agency. . . ."

"Why exclude her, though?" asked Paulina, **shaking** her snout.

Colette and Violet consoled their new friend, who had tears in her eyes. She

couldn't find the **strength** to defend herself.

Onstage, Frau Fledermaus was trying to reason with Signor Mousetti. "This mouselet was admitted thanks to her **video** audition. Her talent is at the same level as the others. There's nothing in the rules that would prevent her from participating —"

"Well, I'll prevent her!" Signor Mousetti SHOUTED, interrupting her. "We can't admit just any rat, gerbil, or hamster — it brings down the level of competition! Without formal training, she will never blossom into a true ballerina."

"But hard work and PASSION aren't found exclusively in prestigious schools," came a squeak from the audience. Everyone **turned** to see who had spoken.

It was Violet! The other Thea Sisters looked at her with pride. Usually Violet was TIMID and shy, but **INJUSTICE** made her bolder than a bobcat in a bird preserve.

"Carlotta has worked hard, just like everyone else in this room. You can't exclude her before you see her dance," she continued. "She has the heart of a true *ballerina*!"

The theater erupted in applause. Violet's words had hit home with all the ratlings and mouselets who had dedicated themselves to the dream of one day dancing on this famouse stage.

Signor Mousetti seemed **IMPRESSED** by

Violet's conviction. "Very well, she . . . she's admitted," he **stuttered**. He turned to Carlotta and raised one paw in warning. "But I'm keeping an **EYE** on you, young rodent! Make sure you live up to our **high** expectations."

Then he **LOOKED** at his pocket watch, as if he were late for something, and vanished backstage like a **FLASH**. The other judges followed him.

BALLET

Ballet began during the Italian Renaissance, where it developed as entertainment for aristocrats. It quickly spread to France, throughout Europe, and to Russia. By the twentieth century, its appeal had spread to people of all classes and stations. For example, the famous Russian ballerina Agrippina Yakovlevna Vaganova (1879–1951) was the daughter of an usher in the Mariinsky Theatre in St. Petersburg. She created a teaching method that was adopted in many schools internationally. Today, the Vaganova method is an invaluable resource for teachers and dance lovers everywhere.

Carlotta turned to Violet. "I don't know how to thank you! This is the happiest day of my life."

Many other competitors *rushed* over to congratulate Carlotta. They were true dance *lovers*, and they were happy to see her SUCCEED.

Only the five dancers from the agency didn't join the well-wishers; in fact, they seemed annoyed by Carlotta's sudden popularity.

The Thea Sisters left the theater beaming, but Paulina brought everyone back to earth. "That went well, thanks to Violet. But after that *scene* with Signor Mousetti, we have a new name to add to our list of suspects. . . ."

ALL FULL!

That afternoon, the Thea Sisters and their friends **returned** to La Scala. Rehearsals for the competition would begin the next day, and the **dancers** were eager to practice.

However, someone seemed determined to make it **difficult** for the competitors. Only rodents from *Mice for Dance* were allowed to use the practice room. The French choreographer, Maurice Le Bars, **BLOCKED** the mouselets and their friends from entering.

"I'm sorry, you can't go in," Monsieur Le Bars **HiSSeD**.

Paulina was **startled**. She'd heard that voice before!

Vasily **sprang** forward. "What do you mean, we can't?" he protested. "We have to **practice**, too!"

"I **understand**," Monsieur Le Bars responded, pretending to be **sympathetic**. "But this room is reserved for those who are performing first."

Pyotr clenched his fists, ready to **FIGHT**.

Madame Rattlova **STOPPED** him. "It's okay, Pyotr. La Scala has two rooms for rehearsal, so I'm sure we'll find space downstairs."

The group took the **elevator** to the practice room. "I recognized that squeak, **mouselets**!" Paulina whispered. "Monsieur Le Bars was one of the rodents whispering backstage!"

Maurice Le Bars

"They must want to **STOP** us from practicing so the competitors from Mice for Dance will get aHeaD!" Nicky said.

When they reached the second practice room, they got MORE bad news. "My apologies, but this room is all full," Madame Mousekaya warned them.

Madame Rattlova tried to iNSiST, but she had to give in when she saw inside the room. It was so **PACKED** with dancers that they had to take turns using the barre!

"Of course it's already full," Pyotr commented **UNHAPPILY** as they walked AWAY. "Everyone who was chased away from the other practice room is here!"

"I think I recognized her squeak, too!" Colette remarked to Paulina.

Olga Mousekaya

Her friend nodded: The female rodent they had heard **plotting** backstage was definitely Madame Mousekaya!

"What are we going to do now?" Pam groaned. The idea of having to PERFORM without practicing made her whiskers quiver in terror.

"No worries!" Carlotta exclaimed. "La Scala is FULL of places to practice. The backstage area is as laRGe as the stage itself, so we can go there and no one will disturb us."

But yet another JUDGE was lying in wait for them backstage.

"I'm sorry," Robert Smithrat said. "We're setting up the scenery, so this area is off-limits." Then he raised an EYEBROW. "Ask Enrico Mousetti to make room for you on the main stage. He's rehearsing there with the **official** ballet corps, but I'm sure that he'd be happy to accommodate you." Then he walked off, **snickering**.

"Wait, don't tell me," Vasily said. "You recognize his **squeak**, too: Another one of the judges you heard plotting backstage."

The Thea Sisters nodded with a **sigh**. Carlotta looked confused, so the mouselets told their new **friend** about their suspicions. "But that's terrible!" Carlotta cried.

Seeing all the young mice so **down** in the snout, Madame Rattlova realized that there was something more important than rehearsing at that moment: **BOOSTING** their spirits!

Robert Smithrat

The Thea Sisters recognized the voices of the three judges who were plotting backstage: Monsieur Le Bars, Madame Mousekaya, and Mr. Smithrat! All three are making it difficult for the dancers to practice. Could they be working with Mice for Dance?

THE CITY IS OUR STAGE!

The Thea Sisters, Vasily, Pyotr, and Carlotta collapsed on benches in the square in front of the theater.

"On your paws!" Madame Rattlova urged them. "A true artist doesn't need a special place to practice his or her craft!"

Her two nephews didn't seem to share her **enthusiasm**.

"You want us to practice . . . here, outside?!" Pyotr replied with dismay.

"But there's a constant **stream** of dancers going in and out of the most **famouse** theater in the world!" Vasily said, looking around nervously. "I'd be too **embarrassed** to set paw on a real

stage after practicing out on the street!"

"Do you even hear the words you're squeaking?" Pam said, shooting the two ratlings her sternest look. "This is no time to act HIGH AND MIGHTY!"

"Pam's right," Nicky agreed. "We've got a mission to accomplish. We can't let those NASTY rodents from Mice for Dance win!"

"If they don't let us practice at La Scala," Paulina continued, "then we'll use the city!"

Colette clapped enthusiastically. "Great idea! Milan will be our *stage*!"

Madame Rattlova nodded approvingly: That was the right spirit!

Carlotta had an idea. "I know where we can GO! Just a few Metro stops away, there's a PARK that would be perfect for us."

Violet turned to the two cousins, who were still **sulking**. "Aren't you coming?"

The two ratlings looked embarrassed that Violet had caught them moping. They LEAPED to their paws.

Violet and Pam linked paws with the cousins. "FRIENDS TOGETHER, MICE FOREVER!" they exclaimed.

The group quickly formed a long chain. The eight DANCERS walked happily, doing little dance steps along the way.

No one noticed the mysterious figure shadowing them as they left the piazza.

To get to the Metro, they passed through the elegant Galleria Vittorio Emanuele II, which **CHARMED** Colette with its beautiful marble columns and sparkling lights.

Pam headed straight for a store that sold gelato in every flavor. It was a true *Italian*

specialty that was whisker-licking delicious!

When they reached the square in front of the Duomo — the cathedral — Paulina pulled out her camera and started taking photographs. She wanted to remember each and every one of the cathedral's spectacular GARGOYLES.

Then they headed to Sforza Castle. After the **CROWDED** Metro, the square in front of the castle, with its enormouse FOUNTAIN, was a peaceful oasis. They walked beyond the walls, past the **massive** building, and arrived at Sempione Park.

"You were right about this place!" Nicky sighed, **beaming**, as she skipped around in a circle.

Pam found a group of **drummers** practicing in a small amphitheater. Soon she started DANCING along to the beat,

THE CITY AS STAGE!

 What a fabumouse afternoon for the Thea Sisters! But someone has been following them ... do you see him?

If you can't find him, the answer is waiting for you on page 74.

dragging Vasily along with her.

Finally, they all gathered in a small, empty paved area, and practiced steps under the careful watch of Madame Rattlova and a few interested passersby. How **wonderful** to be dancing out in the open air!

Colette, Nicky, Pam, Paulina, Violet, Carlotta, Pyotr, and Vasily practiced all day long. It was a day filled with laughter, sweat, and hard work. By *sunset*, the eight dancers were exhausted, but closer to one another than ever.

"Living, breathing, practicing . . . that's the formula for becoming a GREAT dancer!" Madame Rattlova said to herself. She smiled SLYLY. "Mice for Dance's tricks have helped us, not hurt us!"

A SPY IN THE SHADOWS

The Thea Sisters squeaked good-bye to **Carlotta**, who went home for dinner. Then they *hurried* back to their hotel for their own supper. After all that exercise, they were HUNGRIER than a pack of cats at feeding time.

When they reached the hotel restaurant, they found the other DANCERS from the competition sitting together at a noisy, colorful table. The mouselets joined them. Nicky befriended two fellow Aussies, while Violet chatted with a **CHINESE** mouselet who was studying dance in Beijing.

The mouselets were enjoying their pleasant conversation. But as soon as Vasily and Pyotr joined the group, they started **bickering** about different theories of DANCE. According to Vasily, dancers needed to be open to influences from all around the world in order to **grow**.

Pyotr, though, insisted that the only way to learn *ballet* was to follow the traditions of the *Russian* school. Each cousin was convinced that he was right.

Then Nicky **INTERRUPTED**. "I don't see the dancers from Mice for Dance," she remarked. "Aren't they eating with us?"

This new subject got everyone **FIRED** up!

"How rude!" said a Belgian dancer.

"I heard they were invited to a **film** premiere, and then they're going to the opening of a new **NIGHTCLUB**," one of the

Australian dancers reported.

Violet's new Chinese friend **shook** her snout. "They're very good, but how can they perform well if they're out **partying** all night?"

"It's **STRANGE**, don't you think?" Paulina commented. "During the competition they should stay in and **rest**, not go out!"

"Unless they're sure they'll win . . ." Colette whispered in reply.

After dinner, the **THEA SISTERS' SUSPICIONS** were confirmed. As they were waiting for the elevator, they ran into Gaspard Roditeur, who was dressed very elegantly. He was returning to his room to change clothes before heading out to his next shindig. He looked tired — he had circles under his eyes — but he was just as **arrogant** as ever.

"Hi there!" he winked at Colette. "Care to join me at a new NIGHTCLUB?"

Colette smiled politely. "Sorry, Gaspard," she said. "I've got to save my DANCE steps for the competition."

Gaspard waved a paw carelessly. "Oh, that! No worries, I've got that all sewn up."

"Yes, yes, so we hear," Colette replied, rolling her eyes. She joined her friends in the elevator. "You and your friends will be the stars of the show, yadda yadda yadda. . . ."

The elevator doors closed, and Gaspard was left staring at them in surprise. He wasn't

used to being treated so dismissively. As he **TURNED** to go, a paw reached out and **STOPPED** him.

"Who is — ?!" he exclaimed. Then he recognized the figure in the SHADOWS and approached it cautiously. "Oh, it's you."

The *mysterious* squeaker **STEPPED** back into the shadows.

"I **followed** those **mouselets** all day. They have a reputation for poking their snouts where they don't belong. You must give us a paw and make some trouble for them!"

The spy who followed the Thea Sisters knows Gaspard Roditeur! Who could it be? And why would he want to make trouble for the mouselets?

REVEALING PHOTOS

Meanwhile, back in their room, the Thea Sisters were **RELAXING**, thinking over their fabumouse afternoon. Paulina had uploaded some **photos** onto her laptop, and everyone gathered around to take a look.

"**LOOK**, Pam!" Nicky giggled. "That

gelato is bigger than you are!"

"The Duomo is so beautiful!" Paulina continued, moving **forward** through the pictures. "And the park . . ."

Suddenly, Violet grew serious. "Hey! Stop for a sec. Can you *ZOOM* in on that picture?"

Paulina nodded and **clicked** on the image her friend had indicated.

Violet studied the photo for a few seconds,

DO YOU SEE THE MYSTERIOUS RODENT WHO'S BEEN FOLLOWING THE MOUSELETS?

scrunching up her snout in concentration. Finally, she nodded and pointed to the screen.

"Do you see that rodent in the hat? This is going to sound strange, but I think we've seen him before."

"Hmm . . . you're right!" Pam exclaimed. "He was in front of the castle, too!"

"And I noticed him at the park," Colette added.

Paulina **quickly** pulled up all the photographs. The same short **RODENT** wearing a hat and a **heavy** trench coat was in **each** picture!

"Who could it be?" Colette asked.

"Something tells me that Mice for Dance has a **PAW** in all this," Violet said.

"Hit the brakes," Pam said. "First they **prevented** us from entering the practice rooms, and now they're **FOLLOWING** us?!"

"We definitely need to watch our pawsteps," Paulina said thoughtfully. "The three judges we recognized might not be the only ones working with them."

Nicky shook her snout. "Mouselets, this **stinks** worse than Limburger cheese."

"Madame Rattlova was right: They'll do **anything** to win!" Colette concluded.

The mouselets suspect that someone from Mice for Dance has been following them. Do you think they're right?

MADAME RATTLOVA'S CHOICE

The next morning, the mouselets were up and ready in RECORD time. They were among the first to arrive at the rehearsal room.

Madame Rattlova welcomed them with a **BIG** smile. "This time, those crooked judges can't play TRICKS on us," she reassured them. "Today's schedule includes rehearsal of the required steps, and all participants must be present. No exceptions!"

Signor Mousetti himself OPENED the doors and stood at the front of the room, scrutinizing the little crowd of dancers.

When all the performers had taken their places in front of the mirror, the warm-up exercises began. The THEA SISTERS were nervous and jittery. Violet was the only one who seemed at ease: Her arms formed beautiful **arcs** in the air, and she **stretched** her long legs effortlessly.

Madame Rattlova studied her every **move**, nodding with satisfaction. *Violet is truly graceful*, she thought.

Colette and Carlotta were next to each other at the BARRE, and the other dancers thought they were seeing double.

The two **mouselets** had accidentally

dressed alike, and they looked like identical **twins**!

"Whoa, what a resemblance!" Pam said. "They even chose the same fur-do!"

Colette thought it was funny that they looked so similar. She began imitating Carlotta's movements, so it was almost like LOOKING at herself in a mirror! This spurred her to perform better than ever, which Madame Rattlova noted.

After a few more minutes, Madame Rattlova announced, "Violet will partner with Pyotr, and Vasily will DANCE with Colette in the *pas de deux**."

Colette smiled *triumphantly*. She was pleased at having been chosen to dance with one of Madame Rattlova's star pupils. Violet blushed bright **RED**. She hated being the center of attention.

---

* *Pas de deux* means "steps for two." It refers to a piece in which a male dancer and female dancer perform together.

PUFF ... PUFF ...

Then it was time to practice figures. **Small** groups of dancers took turns performing in the middle of the room.

The first competitors took their positions. At first, they practiced slow, sustained movements. As the rehearsal continued, their steps became more dynamic and complex — from small jumps and *glissades** to more **difficult** jumps.

When it was their turn, the Thea Sisters gave it their all, but the technical skill of the other dancers was high, and the mouselets were soon out of **breath**.

"Not bad . . . *puff* . . . *puff* . . . especially since we're really here to investigate," Pam panted. "My pistons are really pumping now!"

---

* *Glissade* means "slide," and usually is a step done in preparation for a more complex figure or a jump.

Violet and Colette were working **HARD**, but when it was time for their first grand jump, their legs were each **trembling** with effort.

Carlotta, on the other paw, was holding her own. Her **grace**, agility, and form were remarkable. She was undoubtedly the best at each sequence of moves. Soon the other **DANCERS** had begun studying her movements in the mirror.

"She's the real **CHEESE**," Nicky said admiringly, watching their new friend.

The dancers from Mice for Dance seemed particularly interested in Carlotta. They watched from across the room, **scowling**.

As for Madame Rattlova, she was as proud as if Carlotta were one of her students. When there is talent and **passion**, true dancers recognize it!

Even Signor Mousetti had started to observe Carlotta more closely. Was he changing his mind about this self-taught ballerina?

Suddenly, a murmur of admiration ECHOED through the room: "Oooohhhh!"

Carlotta had just performed a jump followed by a spin and a scissor-leap in midair. Then she landed on her toes, LIGHT as a butterfly.

Every rodent in the rehearsal room was STUNNED. It was quieter than the library at Mouseford Academy the night before final exams. Until . . .

"What a magnificent *jeté entrelacé**!" Olga Mousekaya **burst** out. Then she clapped a paw over her mouth: She was supposed to support the competitors from Mice for Dance, not give compliments to RIVAL dancers!

But the *jeté entrelacé* required great mastery, and not many DANCE STUDENTS were capable of **executing** it with such grace.

Even Signor Mousetti was squeakless. Madame Rattlova took the opportunity to APPROACH him. "Now that you've seen this mouselet perform, what do you think?" she prodded him.

Jeté entrelacé is from the French: *jeté* means "thrown," and *entrelacé* means "intertwined." It's one of the variations on the jumping dance step called *jeté*.

Mousetti **SCOWLED** at her. "We shall see tomorrow, Madame!"

Then he **checked** his watch and added, "Remember, we will begin at nine o'clock sharp. I do not tolerate lateness." With that, he threw back his tail and **STALKED** out of the room.

As soon as he had gone, Robert Smithrat signaled to Maurice Le Bars, who exchanged a **LOOK** with Gaspard Roditeur.

Paulina raised an eyebrow at Colette. She couldn't help wondering if those three were up to something **shady**. . . .

THE WRONG
BALLERINA

The dancers moved on to the last phase of the rehearsal session: jumps and lifts. For this exercise, each ballerina did a few small **LEAPS** until she reached a ratling partner, who would grab her by the waist and lift her to complete the jump. Then he would **gently** return her to the floor.

Gaspard Roditeur couldn't take his **EYES** off Carlotta. Nicky noticed and smiled. "Look!" she WHiSPeReD to Pam. "Apparently even Gaspard is **impressed** by her talent!"

The mouselets started to **line up** in front of their partners. Carlotta was about to take her turn when she realized that the ribbons of her toe shoe were untied, so she asked Colette to go instead.

When Gaspard saw a mouselet with a blonde braid come forward, he swept aside his **FELLOW** dancers.

Colette performed her final **LEAP** and found herself snout-to-snout with Gaspard. The ratling took hold of her waist, lifted her into the air like a delicate **SLICE** of Swiss, and brought her back to the floor — **HEAVILY**, like a huge block of cheddar!

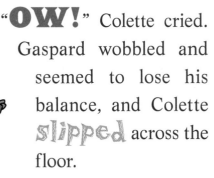

"**OW!**" Colette cried. Gaspard wobbled and seemed to lose his balance, and Colette slipped across the floor.

Nicky, Pam, Paulina,

Violet, and Madame Rattlova *hurried* to help her, but Colette's ankle was already **swollen**. She was injured. For her, the competition was over!

"**OH!** I'm so sorry. . . ." Gaspard said loudly.

Nicky shot him an angry look. He didn't seem that sorry to her.

She was still glaring at him an instant later, when Carlotta *RAN* to Colette's side. The smirk on Gaspard's snout turned into a look of **Confusion** and dismay.

"Did you see that?" Nicky WHiSPEReD to Paulina, who was next to her. "I think he did it on purpose! Gaspard got Colette and Carlotta confused — he **INJURED** the *wrong* ballerina!"

Paulina nodded grimly. "You're right, Nic. But, shh, here come the judges!"

The judges **working** with the agency had rushed over to examine Colette.

"Call the **doctor!**" Madame Mousekaya ordered. "This rehearsal session is over."

Once they were safely in the dressing room, the **THEA SISTERS** shared their suspicions about Gaspard and tried to cheer up their friend.

"Snout up, Coco," Pamela sighed. "At least now you can get a little *rest*. . . ."

"If you take it easy, you might still be able to participate in the **gala**," Violet added.

Madame Rattlova entered in a **FURY**. "This is unheard of! I've made an official complaint, but unfortunately we can't prove that it wasn't an *accident*," she sighed.

Colette was MOVED by all this kindness, but there was one thing that consoled her more than anything: Carlotta was safe. She could still make her **dream** come true!

"You'll see, in a few days I'll be back on my paws," she said, winking. "And now I'll have more time to *investigate*!"

THE FIRST AUDITION

The next day, **OFFICIAL** auditions began. The rodents gathered in the rehearsal room were **TENSER** than rats in a cat clinic. All the dancers were concentrating hard.

The Thea Sisters felt like they were on **Pins and needles**. They were too nervous to talk to one another. Even chatty Pam stayed silent for the whole **WARM—UP**!

The only calm one was Colette, who was seated next to the door with her ankle wrapped. She waved to her friends with a smile, **WINKING** to encourage them.

Suddenly, the room fell **absolutely** silent: The six

judges had entered and were heading for a long table in the back of the room. Signor Mousetti was the last in line. The expression on his snout was **SEVERE** as he checked the TIME on his watch. When it struck nine on the dot, he nodded to Frau Fledermaus, the Austrian judge. She pulled out a list of the candidates and started to read the DANCERS' names.

The five rodents from *Mice for Dance* were the first to be called. Gaspard Roditeur positioned himself in the middle of the room, waiting for the first chords from the piano. Then he began his performance.

Gaspard's physical **STRENGTH** put a spring in his pawstep when he jumped, but his form was ROUGH in places. His audition was less than satisfactory.

The judges working with Mice for Dance

did everything they could to INFLUENCE their colleagues. Robert Smithrat whispered in Signor Mousetti's ear the whole time, squeaking the praises of his protégé. "What style, what powerful EXPRESSION!"

Mousetti nodded, but his expression remained unreadable.

Thanks to overly generous scores from Monsieur Le Bars, Mr. Smithrat, and

Madame Mousekaya, the votes went in favor of Gaspard and the other dancers from *Mice for Dance*.

But the **comments** from these three judges were anything but positive when it came time for the other dancers to perform. Every little imperfection became an offense to the purity of dance. Their votes **HEAVILY** influenced the other judges, and of the Thea Sisters, only **Violet** made it past the first round.

The mouselets didn't mind, though, and **congratulated** their friend.

"You're so amazing, Vi!" Paulina said, hugging her.

"I must go thank Sir Geoffrey Gopherson," Violet said SHYLY. "It's only thanks to his generous score that I **passed**! But it's a **SHAME** that we won't all be performing together tomorrow. . . ."

"Yeah," Pam agreed. "But I must confess: I'm relieved! I've been so **stressed** about dancing since we arrived in Milan."

Just then, Frau Fledermaus called out the next dancer: "Carlotta Ratignani, come forward!"

JUSTICE IS SERVED

It was the moment they had been waiting for. All eyes were on Carlotta as she moved to the center of the room.

Since she was a little mouseling, Carlotta had been secretly watching dancers rehearse before the mirrors of the La Scala practice room. And now *she* was the ballerina reflected in the mirror!

When the first notes of the piano echoed in the air, the MOVES that she had practiced thousands of times took shape with grace and the look of *effortlessness*.

Everyone watching her fell under her spell. Her DANCING was really something special.

Robert Smithrat was stunned. He immediately began muttering in Enrico

Mousetti's ear, hoping to distract him from Carlotta's performance. "This mouselet is **IMMATURE**. She may jump well, but—"

"Robert, please **shut your snout**!" Signor Mousetti hissed.

The famouse choreographer didn't miss a single one of Carlotta's moves. For a few moments his normally scowling expression SOFTENED into something like a **smile**!

The judges working with the agency exchanged a worried **LOOK**. They had planned to influence Mousetti, but now that they saw his reaction to Carlotta's audition, their best hope was that their low scores would **DISQUALIFY** her from the competition.

When Carlotta finished, she gave a slight bow. Spontaneous applause **BURST** out from the other competitors, and the three impartial judges nodded vigorously. Their scores were high, while the judges **working** with the agency gave her a chilly response.

When Carlotta's scores were read, a *confused* murmur went up around the room.

"But . . ." Paulina murmured, quickly adding up the scores. "Carlotta will be CUT from the competition!"

The Thea Sisters began to tremble with indignation: This was unfair!

"Just a moment!" Signor Mousetti's squeak echoed *loud* and CLEAR through the room. "The scores that were just read don't do justice to this performance." The elderly choreographer stood up and **LOOKED** reproachfully at the three judges who had given Carlotta low scores.

"As president of the jury, my vote is worth

DOUBLE," he continued. "And I intend to give this **young** ballerina the maximum number of points. Her skill is so great that she officially passes to the next round!"

"Hooray!" The dance students gave Signor Mousetti's declaration a standing ovation.

The Thea Sisters **SCURRIED** over to congratulate **Carlotta**, who couldn't believe everything that had just happened!

Maurice Le Bars caught the **EYES** of Robert Smithrat and Olga Mousekaya, who nodded at him. It was time to intervene.

Monsieur Le Bars motioned to Gaspard Roditeur. "I need to squeak with you," he whispered.

? AN IMPORTANT CLUE

The first **day** of the competition had ended. Madame Rattlova's group reunited in the hallway to **celebrate** Violet, Carlotta, and the two cousins. Pyotr and Vasily had performed earlier in the day and had passed, in spite of the **unfair** low scores from the three **CROOKED** judges.

"You know, cousin," Vasily whispered to Pyotr, "I hate to admit it, but when you dance, you're no **moldy** cheese."

Pyotr smiled. "Thanks, cousin. You're not so bad yourself!"

"Did you see that

unbelievable favoritism?" Paulina spluttered. "**THANK GOODMOUSE** Signor Mousetti fought against Carlotta's elimination. Maybe now we can take him off the list of suspects."

Violet nodded **thoughtfully** and added, "It seems like Sir Geoffrey Gopherson, Frau Fledermaus, and Mr. Sasaku aren't part of the **PLOT**, either. Their scores seemed fair."

"Do you think the other **judges** will interfere in the next round of auditions?" asked Carlotta, looking worried.

"I think I know someone who could tell

THE HONEST JUDGES

MARTHA FLEDERMAUS KOICHI SASAKU SIR GEOFFREY GOPHERSON

us," Colette responded with a sly SMILE. She turned around and LIMPED away from the group. "Wait here, I'll be right back!"

The others followed her with their eyes as she tapped Gaspard Roditeur's shoulder.

The dancer turned around. As soon as he recognized her, he **blushed** from the tip of his snout to the tip of his tail.

"Check it out!" Pam commented. "It looks like Colette is turning on her **CHARM**!"

Colette and Gaspard squeaked rapidly in French for a few minutes. Then he

THE CORRUPT JUDGES

ROBERT SMITHRAT

OLGA MOUSEKAYA

MAURICE LE BARS

ENRICO MOUSETTI

KISSED her paw, and Colette turned back to her friends, **beaming**.

"**Incredible!**" Paulina said. "You wiped the snooty look right off his snout. What did you say to him?"

"Oh, nothing!" Colette said airily. "I just gave him a compliment, and he **melted** like mozzarella on a hot summer's day."

Pam and Paulina giggled.

"Unfortunately," Colette **sighed**, "Gaspard

didn't say anything about the agency's plans. But he did boast about how he's going to be the lead DANCER at the Paris Opera!"

"Oh, sure, because getting that GIG is a total piece of cheesecake!" Vasily scoffed.

"He is ONE HUNDRED PERCENT sure that he'll get the job!" Colette continued. "He says Monsieur Le Bars is meeting him tonight to make an official offer."

"Impossible!" Madame Rattlova cried. "The international community would never accept a SCAM like this!"

Violet said aloud what everyone was thinking. "But if we could record their conversation, we'd have the PROOF we need to unmask these CROOKED judges!"

Colette found out about Gaspard Roditeur's secret appointment with Monsieur Le Bars. Is the choreographer really planning to offer him a job?

SPLITTING UP

That evening, after a refreshing shower and a ratnap, the mouselets and the two cousins met in the hotel lobby.

The **THEA SISTERS** were determined to follow through on their plan: They would **SECRETLY** follow Gaspard Roditeur to his appointment so they could record his conversation with Monsieur Le Bars.

"We're going to stick to him closer than a glue trap," Pam declared.

"That's right," Paulina said, holding up her **CAMERA**. "We won't let him out of our sight. If all goes well, we'll catch those two crooks on candid camera."

"Finally, a little ***action***!" Vasily exclaimed. He turned to Violet. "Don't

WORRY, I'll be close by if you need help. . . ."

Faster than a cat with a ball of yarn, Pyotr sprang to Violet's side. "Don't get your tail in a twist, cousin," he said. "Violet is my *partner* in the *pas de deux*, so I'll take care of her!"

After the first audition, the two rivals seemed to have reached a truce, but not

when it came to affairs of the **HeaRt**!

Violet took matters into her own paws. "That's enough!" she said, exasperated. "I don't need two ratlings fighting over who's going to save me, okay?! If I need help, I'll go to my friends: the **THEA SiSTERS**!"

"You said it, sister!" Pam applauded.

An **AMUSED** squeak came from behind them. "Besides, you two cheeseheads aren't going anywhere tonight!"

Curious, all the mice turned around.

It was Madame Rattlova. She and Carlotta were approaching the little group.

"Tomorrow will be a BUSY day for you and your partners," the teacher continued. "Carlotta will take Colette's place, and all four of you are **shaky** on the *pas de deux.* You need to practice in pairs if you want to have any hope of **winning**!"

"My mother squeaked with the doorman at LA SCALA and convinced him to let us in," Carlotta added. She was *happy* to be able to help her new friends. "Tonight we can rehearse on the **MAIN** stage!"

Violet and the two cousins were so excited, they almost jumped out of their fur.

"HOLEY CHEESE!" Pyotr exclaimed. "What an honor!"

So the group split up: Carlotta, Violet, and the cousins RETURNED to La Scala to rehearse, Colette reluctantly went back to the hotel room to rest her ankle, and Pam, Nicky, and Paulina got ready to follow Gaspard Roditeur.

THE CHASE WAS ON!

A SECRET MEETING
... WITH A TWIST!

Right after dinner, Gaspard Roditeur left the hotel. The Thea Sisters were ready to follow him all over Milan if necessary.

Gaspard headed toward the Duomo and then onto a large, **BUSY** street. The mouselets followed him, but it was difficult keeping track of him in the crowd. *Nicky*, PAMELA, and PAULINA looked around frantically, afraid they were going to lose him.

Luckily, after a moment or two, Nicky spotted him going through a large archway.

The mouselets cautiously **SCURRIED** after him. If he was going into an apartment building, it would be impossible to *film* him!

But when they passed under the arch, they were surprised to find themselves in a deserted square surrounded by four walls. The **quiet** atmosphere felt strange after the crowded street they'd just left.

"This is an *amazing* place!" Pam murmured. "It's like a piece of the medieval world dropped into modern times!"

Paulina **dusted** off her guidebook to

Milan. "We're in the Piazza Mercanti, the ancient commercial **heart** of the city. This is where rich merchants met to conduct BUSINESS and arrange secret deals."

Nicky looked around. "I don't SEE Gaspard anymore," she whispered.

The ratling seemed to have vanished into thin air! The mouselets carefully scanned the square until they heard **pawsteps** in the distance. Then they caught sight of the dancer. He was standing behind a large pillar, talking with a short rodent in a **LARGE** hat and a **DARK** trench coat.

"I don't believe it!" Nicky whispered. "Do you see that mouse? He's the one who followed us the first day of rehearsals!"

Paulina, Nicky, and Pam looked at one another.

"We've definitely seen that rodent at La Scala!" Pam confirmed.

LET'S REVIEW THE SITUATION:

- The agency Mice for Dance bribes judges and fixes competitions so its dancers always win.
- There are at least three judges on the competition jury who are working with the agency.
- Those three judges have done everything they can to eliminate the best dancers.
- A mysterious rodent has been following the Thea Sisters and Carlotta.
- The "accident" with Gaspard and Colette seems to have been part of the agency's plan.
- Monsieur Le Bars arranged for a meeting with Gaspard, perhaps to guarantee him a prestigious job.
- Gaspard is meeting with the same mysterious rodent who was following the Thea Sisters.

SCHEMING
IN THE PIAZZA

At last, the mouselets got a good **LOOK** at the rodent who'd been following them. The viewfinder of their camera revealed his identity. It was **Maurice Le Bars**!

"If only we could hear what they're saying," Paulina moaned. The two conspirators were MURMURING to each other under the protection of the columns that ran along one side of the piazza.

The mouselets tried to inch a little closer, but with each step they risked being discovered.

Pam held up her paw to stop the others. "We can't get any closer or they'll see us."

Nicky leaned on a column, **disappointed**.

That's when something amazing happened: She could **HEAR** Monsieur Le Bars squeaking!

The *French* judge's words reached her clearly and PRECISELY. "**Mousetti** is unpredictable, so we can't make any more **MISTAKES.** We need to get **RID** of Carlotta Ratignani, understand?"

Nicky's eyes opened wide. She **quickly gestured** to her friends to come closer.

Pamela and Paulina **HEADED** for where Nicky was standing. When they stood next to one of the columns, they could distinctly hear Monsieur Le Bars's **squeak**, even though he was at least thirty feet away! But how?

"Wait a minute, I read about this!" Paulina recalled, flipping through the pages of her **GUIDEBOOK**. "The **arches** inside this piazza were constructed to transmit sound!"

"How convenient for **SNEAKY** medieval merchants conducting business on the **SLY**!" Pam said.

"And for us, too!" Nicky added.

So the Thea Sisters were able to listen in on the whole conversation between Le Bars and **GASPARD**. It turned out that the judge hadn't arranged this meeting to offer him a job as lead dancer. In fact, the purpose of the meeting was far more **WICKED**!

"I don't care how you do it, but you must **STOP** that interfering Italian ballerina,"

Le Bars WHISPERED. "Tomorrow, Carlotta Ratignani must not arrive on time!"

"But I won't be able to **delay** her for more than a few minutes," Gaspard objected. He sounded **uncomfortable** with what Monsieur Le Bars was asking.

"Don't worry your little snout about that," Monsieur Le Bars replied. "You'll see — five minutes will be enough to **disqualify** her from the competition. We'll arrange for Mousetti's watch to show the 'correct' time! He's so strict that he won't bend the rules, not even for even a second. **Hee, hee, hee!**"

Nicky, Pam, and Paulina looked at one another. They had to restrain themselves from jumping in right then. What a bunch of **crooks**!

A NEW ALLY

Meanwhile, back at the theater, Madame Rattlova's DANCERS were practicing their paws off.

"No, Pyotr, not like that!" the teacher exclaimed. "You're too early for Violet!"

Onstage, her students were sweaty and EXHAUSTED, but they didn't intend to stop until they had perfected their routine.

"Come on," Violet said, smiling at her partner. "Let's start again!"

Pyotr's ears DROOPED with exhaustion. "I'm sorry, Violet. I just can't seem to make snouts or tails of these last few steps!"

Vasily grinned. "Maybe you're not putting your best paw forward, cuz."

Pyotr shot him a dirty look. But then he

understood the real reason for the teasing: to shake him out of his **SLUMP**. The two cousins really did CARE about each other!

"Here," Vasily continued, taking his cousin's paw, "let's practice: one, two . . ."

The two ratlings **moved** together, matching their steps perfectly, as if their hearts were beating with the same rhythm. It was an inspiring SIGHT.

Madame Rattlova watched them proudly, while Violet and Carlotta smiled.

Those two cousins were like brothers, united by their talent and their **love** for dance!

Violet heard Carlotta's voice behind her. "Exciting, isn't it?"

"These are the moments that make all the sacrifices worth it," Violet agreed.

Her friend LAUGHED happily. "At night, my legs ache, and my paws rebel against my toe shoes. But I wouldn't trade those feelings for anything in the world!"

"Good for you, young mouselet!" The unmistakable squeak of Enrico Mousetti echoed from the SHADOWS. The **old** choreographer often remained in the theater after it closed. After so many years, he felt at home there.

The dancers **froze**. Madame Rattlova moved forward, afraid that the strict judge would scold them, but he reassured her.

"I've been **WATCHING** you for a while from the audience. The only reason I stepped forward is because I'd like to say something."

He strode toward the stage and addressed Carlotta. "I must apologize, **miss**," he said seriously. "Watching you and your friends rehearse with such *passion*, I've realized how **out-of-date** some of my opinions are. No one deserves to be in this competition more than you do!"

Carlotta twisted her tail timidly. "Thank you, sir."

Violet **smiled**. Maybe they had found a new ally against Mice for Dance!

A PLAN!

Violet looked at Madame Rattlova, who nodded: The moment had come to find out if the old **choreographer** was on their side.

Signor Mousetti approached Madame Rattlova and bent over to kiss her paw with one swift, **elegant** motion. "I admit it, Madame Rattlova. You were right!"

He **praised** her two nephews, and then he turned to Violet.

"My dear, you were the first to doubt my words," he observed. "And with such **confidence**! You **surprised**

me. But you were absolutely right."

Violet BLUSHED at being singled out by the eminent choreographer.

"Thank you, maestro," she began. "There's something very **important** that you need to know."

With the help of Madame Rattlova, Pyotr, Vasily, and Carlotta, Violet told Signor Mousetti EVERYTHING that had happened since they had arrived in Milan: The conversation they had OVERHEARD the first day, how the drawing had been fixed, the ban on practicing in the theater, and all the other **trouble** the three judges from the agency had cooked up.

"That's why Smithrat wouldn't stop yammering in my ear!" Signor Mousetti finally said, shocked. "I can't believe they dared to do it!"

"The agency's plotting isn't limited to this competition," Madame Rattlova added. "Mice for Dance has FIXED all the most important international competitions!"

Signor Mousetti was **scandalized**. "I won't allow those imposters to get the better of us here," he **declared**. "Not at La Scala!"

"You said it, buster!" said a new voice from the audience. "Um, that is . . . Mr. Director!"

It was PAm. Colette, Paulina, and Nicky were right behind her.

Nicky, Pam, and Paulina had returned to the hotel to pick up Colette. Together, the four mouseLets had hurried to the theater to share their news. They needed to come up with a STRATEGY right away!

They told their friends about the conversation between Le Bars and Gaspard, and the plan to eliminate Carlotta from the competition.

"UNfoRtuNateLy, we weren't able to film them, so we still don't have the proof we need," Paulina began.

"But we *do* have a plan!" Nicky put in.

Colette spread her paws and gestured for everyone to huddle up. "With a LittLe help from everyone, tomorrow we'll catch those crooked judges RED-PAWED!"

Everyone turned to Signor Mousetti, anxious to see what he thought.

The old choreographer nodded. "I'm with you!"

SURPRISE ELIMINATION!

The next morning, the Thea Sisters and the other competitors went straight to the **REHEARSAL** room. It was time for the second round of auditions. Colette, Nicky, Pam, and Paulina had already been **eliminated**, but they were there to support **Violet**, who was even more anxious than she had been the day before.

"We haven't practiced enough!" she moaned, *tangling* the ribbons of her toe shoes as she tried to **tie** them.

"You're going to be fabumouse, Vi," Paulina reassured her **sweetly**, fixing her ribbons. "We're all here for you!"

Actually, not all of them were there. One

of the Thea Sisters was **MISSING**: Where was Colette?

At that moment, **Signor Mousetti** strode into the room, with the other judges right behind him.

The **strict** choreographer smiled at Madame Rattlova and **WINKED** at the two cousins. That was their signal: Everything was in place for the Thea Sisters' scheme to *catch* the crooked judges. And Colette's absence was part of the PLAN!

Meanwhile, the three judges from the agency sat down and made themselves COMFORTABLE. They also had a plan, which was to eliminate **Carlotta** from the competition!

Gaspard was more SKITTISH than a kitten in a dog kennel. He couldn't stop adjusting his fur in front of the **mirror**, and he cast apprehensive looks at the judges' table.

Monsieur Le Bars **smiled** at him confidently, but that only seemed to make Gaspard more agitated!

"I feel a little bit sorry for him," Paulina murmured to her friends, watching the young DANCER get ready. "They may have promised him honor and **glory**, but for now, his talent is suffering."

Pam just shook her snout. "Oh, sure, it

must be so hard to be a RAT FINK!
Instead of working his paws off like the rest
of us, he gets to spend his evenings at *fancy*
restaurants and nightclubs."

The auditions finally began, and the first
to perform was Gaspard.

His ***movements*** were as ENERGETIC
as always, but his routine also showed his

limits. Talent is a gift that is perfected with study and constant practice, which was exactly what the ratling didn't have time for once he joined Mice for Dance!

Signor Mousetti's verdict was very severe. "You lack the qualities of a *danseur noble**, my ratling. I recommend that you return to your studies so you can refine your talent before you audition again. In my opinion, your audition today is not at the level required for this competition."

The other judges supported the director's opinion, and no one listened to the PROTESTS of Monsieur Le Bars, Madame Mousekaya, and Mr. Smithrat. In spite of the agency's support, Gaspard Roditeur had been *eliminated*!

Danseur noble is French for "noble dancer," and refers to a principal male dancer who succeeds in expressing control, grace, and sophistication.

PRISONER!

The ratlings' auditions concluded with the triumph of Pyotr and Vasily, who **ended** up at the top of the rankings, both within a few POINTS of each other.

Gaspard stayed in a corner and watched them. After his elimination, he was angry. But he still hoped to get his revenge. He might not have **BEATEN** those two ratlings, but at least he could help eliminate their friend Carlotta!

Meanwhile, the three judges from the agency were squirming in their chairs. They had just lost the prize for the ratlings' division, and they were determined not to lose the mouselets' division, too!

The auditions continued. Next came the ballerinas from Mice for Dance, who won **FAVOR** from the three crooked judges. Then it was **Violet's** turn.

Unfortunately, the last few days had taken their toll on her muscles, and her steps, while they were *graceful* and precise, weren't as expressive as usual. This would only be a small concern back at Mouseford Academy, but it was a serious **PROBLEM** in a prestigious international competition!

"I'm sorry," Signor Mousetti said when she had finished. "Your total score isn't **HIGH** enough for you to continue. But you have **GREAT** talent and I hope to see you again, when you've perfected your technique."

Sir Gopherson, Mr. Sasaku, and Frau Fledermaus agreed with Signor Mousetti's opinion. They nodded and gave Violet a small round of **APPLAUSE**.

Violet returned to her friends with a smile. Even though she hadn't made the cut, she was ***proud*** that she'd given it her all!

Meanwhile, Monsieur Le Bars and Mr. Smithrat exchanged a **sneaky** grin, and Madame Mousekaya commented under her breath, "One down!"

Then the **FRENCH** choreographer motioned to Gaspard. The final stage of their scheme was about to begin!

Gaspard moved to the back of the room and approached Carlotta. Pretending to be **DISTRESSED**, he whispered, "You're Ratignani, right? Your mother is **waiting** for you by the dressing rooms."

Carlotta knew that he wasn't being **honest**, but she pretended to believe him.

"She told me it was **urgent**," he continued. "Come on, I'll go with you!"

Carlotta headed out, with Gaspard on her heels. It was a **quick** trip to the dressing rooms, but Carlotta, who knew the theater like the back of her paw, **SPED** up, putting distance between herself and Gaspard.

"Hey, wait!" he **PROTESTED**.

"But didn't you say it was **urgent**?"

she joked, disappearing into a winding hallway.

The ratling had to **run** to catch up with her. He turned the corner just in time to see a blonde braid DISAPPEAR into the dressing rooms.

Now you're trapped! he **thought** triumphantly, and locked the door behind her.

"Surprised?" he shouted to his PRISONER. "There's no one in there waiting for you,

Gaspard's plan

and I'm not letting you out — not until it's **TOO** late for your audition!"

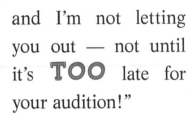

After seeing Carlotta's blonde braid disappear into a dressing room . . .

. . . he hurried to lock the door . . .

. . . and then stood guard in front of it in case anyone tried to let her out!

TiME'S UP!

Back in the rehearsal room, the auditions were almost over. There were just a few names left on Frau Fledermaus's list.

The *ballerina* auditions were dominated by the mouselets from Mice for Dance, but the Thea Sisters weren't **worried**. They were about to put an end to the agency's tricks!

Frau Fledermaus rose to her paws and called out the last name on the list: "Carlotta Ratignani!"

Silence fell over the room. No one stepped forward.

Monsieur Le Bars **snickered**. Everything was going according to **plan**! Signor Mousetti's watch would be the last piece to fall in place.

As the seconds ticked past, the other competitors started to MURMUR with concern.

Robert Smithrat approached Signor Mousetti. "She'll show up, I'm sure of it," he lied. "But, **UNFORTUNATELY**, if she doesn't arrive in the next five minutes . . ."

"Oh, what a disappointment that would be!" Madame Mousekaya interjected, faking a tone of alarm. "In that case, we would be forced to **ELIMINATE** her. . . ."

Signor Mousetti remained serious as he took his faithful watch out of his pocket. "Very well. It's 12:40. We will wait until 12:45."

This was just what Monsieur Le Bars had been expecting. A few moments later, he moved closer to Signor Mousetti. Pretending to **STUMBLE**, he grabbed Mousetti's

paws. "Oops, excuse me!"

Caught by surprise, Mousetti grabbed on to him, letting his **precious** watch fall.

"I'm so sorry!" Monsieur Le Bars apologized, bending down to pick it up. "Please, let me get that."

Before **RETURNING** the watch, he swiftly moved the hands forward to 12:44. Just one more minute and the agency's most **DANGEROUS** rival would be expelled from the competition!

The honest judges — Mr. Sasaku, Sir

Gopherson, and Frau Fledermaus — seemed worried. "Miss Ratignani! It's your turn!" Sasaku called, looking at the door anxiously.

"HERE I AM!" a clear squeak responded from the back of the room.

It was Carlotta. She was back!

Mr. Smithrat THREW Monsieur Le Bars a dirty look, and Madame Mousekaya SPRANG up from her seat, squeakless.

The French choreographer had turned as white as a freshly washed sheet. He looked like he had just come out of the SPIN cycle!

"B-b-but that's n-n-not p-p-poss . . ." he stuttered.

Signor Mousetti and the THEA SiSTERS knew exactly how it was possible: Using the information they had gathered at the Piazza Mercanti, they had foiled the agency's plot! Now Carlotta was here, ready to DANCE.

Robert Smithrat wouldn't give up so easily, though. He took the watch from Signor Mousetti's paws and showed it to everyone.

"Time's up!" he SNAPPED. "It's past 12:45, just look!"

The pocket watch showed that it was already 12:46.

"Oh, my trusty pocket watch must have LOST a few minutes when it fell to the

ground just now," Signor Mousetti replied calmly. With a theatrical gesture, the old choreographer rolled up one of his sleeves, revealing a watch with a *charming* pink wristband (which Colette had loaned him!).

"**Luckily**, I brought an extra watch with me!" he exclaimed with **satisfaction**.

Mr. Smithrat was dumbstruck. Madame Mousekaya fell back into her chair. Monsieur Le Bars **COWERED** like a mouseling who's been cornered by a hungry cat.

"It's 12:43, my dear," Signor Mousetti concluded. "If there are no other objections, you may begin your audition."

TRUTH REVEALED

Now that the three **dishonest** judges' plot had failed, Carlotta could finally perform her solo audition.

The **mouselet** danced with all the **passion** in her heart. Secretly, she was dedicating her steps to everyone who had helped her. Her audition was **EXCELLENT**, and the **TALENTED** ballerina passed with full marks. Even the crooked judges were forced to give her **GOOD** scores, to try to throw off suspicion.

But as soon as the second round of auditions ended, the three **cheaters** leaped to their paws and left in a HURRY.

When they were out of earshot, Smithrat started to yell at Le Bars. "You cheddarhead — you can't even keep a little Italian *ballerina* off her paws?"

"I trusted that cheese puff GASPARD with the task," he replied.

At the dressing rooms, the judges found Gaspard, looking proud as a porcupine as he stood guard in front of the closed door.

"You let that mouselet get away!" Le Bars shouted immediately.

Gaspard stared at them with an open snout. "W-what are you talking about? She's been **trapped** inside all this time!"

"This was the only thing you had to do!" Madame Mousekaya shouted. "We fixed the drawing and gave you high scores, and you're not even capable of keeping a mouselet LOCKED up for two minutes?!"

Gaspard shook his snout in confusion as the *truth* was revealed in a most unexpected way.

"Sorry we had to pull the cheesecloth over your EYES," a quiet squeak interjected. "It's quite simple, you see: I'm not the one you have LOCKED inside that room!"

The three judges and Gaspard turned around in shock. Carlotta was standing behind them, a skeleton KEY in her paw.

A CUЯIOUS crowd was forming behind her, led by the other judges, Signor Mousetti, and the Thea Sisters. The three scam artists had **revealed** themselves in front of many witnesses!

Carlotta opened the door and Colette appeared in the doorway, *smiling*. "So, what score would you give my performance?"

Carlotta and Colette had dressed in *identical* outfits and done their fur in matching 'dos. It had been almost impossible to tell them apart!

"When you lost sight of me, Colette and I **switched** places, and I slipped back to the rehearsal room!" Carlotta explained to a **stunned** Gaspard.

Signor Mousetti stepped forward, looking sternly at the three **crooked** judges. "We let you put your plan into action so that we could catch you in the act. The schemes of *Mice for Dance* are over — forever."

GALA EVENING!

The three corrupt judges were taken into custody, and the DANCERS from Mice for Dance were EXPELLED from the competition. The agency had many associates across the world, but this scandal would ruin them once and for all. It was only a matter of time before they were forced to CLOSE.

Unfortunately, the crooked judges had unfairly influenced the auditions, and the organizers were forced to CANCEL the competition at La Scala.

Signor Mousetti and the three remaining judges gathered the competitors to explain the sudden change.

"We need to redo the entire competition," Mousetti explained over the students'

MURMURS of relief. "This time, we will be much more careful about our jury selection!"

Then he motioned to Madame Rattlova, who **joined** him onstage.

"I am proud to introduce you to one of our new judges," Signor Mousetti said, welcoming her with a **smile**. "This is the famous Madame Natalya Rattlova, the great star of Russian ballet!"

Pyotr and Vasily leaped to their paws and burst into APPLAUSE. The cousins were united by their deep **respect** for their teacher, Madame Rattlova . . . and their **LOVE** for their auntie Natalya!

"Finally, I have some

even more sensational news," Signor Mousetti continued. The room fell SILENT with anticipation. "To make up for the mistakes in the judging, we have decided not to cancel the **gala** performance! It will take place right here onstage at La Scala in Milan and will be BROADCAST all over the world!"

The room shook with applause.

The days that followed were hectic. There

were steps to **rehearse**, costumes to **sew**, and scenery to *arrange*. The MACHINERY backstage at La Scala was put to work!

Each dancer was assigned a role, and the THEA SISTERS had the honor of performing with the young **MASTERS** of the international dance scene.

Violet and Pyotr **performed** their *pas de deux,* and Colette even managed to DANCE with Vasily.

But the real *surprise* of the evening was Carlotta. The critical Milan audience showered her with applause and called her back onstage for **three** bows! The Thea Sisters watched her proudly from behind the scenes: She had been recognized as a true **star**!

A NEW SISTER

It was finally time for the Thea Sisters to return to Mouseford Academy.

The **COMPETITION** participants met in the hotel lobby to say good-bye. Even Signor Mousetti was there! He **thanked** them again for their help.

"It's such a shame that you can't stay for our repeat of the competition," he said. "I'm so glad to have met you!"

Madame Rattlova **hugged** them one by one. "Say hello to my dear friend Professor Ratyshnikov. She has taught you all well!"

Carlotta had tears in her eyes. "Mouselets, you're the **best friends** I could ever ask for! Without you, none of this would have happened!"

Colette gave her a QUICK hug. "To us, you're like a sister now!"

"Don't forget to keep us UPDATED on everything about your career!" Paulina said.

Signor Mousetti had promised to give Carlotta an audition for the ballet corps at La Scala. What an amazing opportunity!

Just then, the two cousins scurried into the lobby with their bags in paw.

"What **LUCK**, you're still here!" Vasily said.

"Aren't you staying for the rest of the competition?" Pam asked, surprised.

"Now that Aunt Natalya is on the jury, we can't participate," Pyotr explained. "I'm going home to *Russia*. There's a lot of work to do for the next *ballet* season."

Vasily had other plans. "There are competitions all over the **world**, and plenty of theaters. I can't wait to visit them all!"

Then he turned to Violet. "I hope to see you again soon," he said. "You can always count on my friendship."

"Mine, too!" Pyotr **interrupted**.

"Thank you," said Violet warmly, and hugged them both.

In their **TAXI** to the airport, Colette couldn't help asking Violet a **NOSY** question. "So, Vi, who did you choose?"

"Choose?" she replied, **mystified**.

"Yes! Vasily or Pyotr?" Pam added.

Violet just laughed. "I thought I already told you! I choose my **faBUmoUSe** friends, the Thea Sisters!"

THEY WERE MORE THAN FRIENDS. THEY WERE SISTERS!

Thea Sisters

Don't miss any of my fabumouse adventures!

Thea Stilton and the Dragon's Code

Thea Stilton and the Mountain of Fire

Thea Stilton and the Ghost of the Shipwreck

Thea Stilton and the Secret City

Thea Stilton and the Mystery in Paris

Thea Stilton and the Cherry Blossom Adventure

Thea Stilton and the Star Castaways

Thea Stilton: Big Trouble in the Big Apple

Thea Stilton and the Ice Treasure

Thea Stilton and the Secret of the Old Castle

Thea Stilton and the Blue Scarab Hunt

Thea Stilton and the Prince's Emerald

Thea Stilton and the Mystery on the Orient Express

Thea Stilton and the Dancing Shadows

Be sure to read these stories, too!

#1 Lost Treasure of the Emerald Eye

#2 The Curse of the Cheese Pyramid

#3 Cat and Mouse in a Haunted House

#4 I'm Too Fond of My Fur!

#5 Four Mice Deep in the Jungle

#6 Paws Off, Cheddarface!

#7 Red Pizzas for a Blue Count

#8 Attack of the Bandit Cats

#9 A Fabumouse Vacation for Geronimo

#10 All Because of a Cup of Coffee

#11 It's Halloween, You 'Fraidy Mouse!

#12 Merry Christmas, Geronimo!

#13 The Phantom of the Subway

#14 The Temple of the Ruby of Fire

#15 The Mona Mousa Code

#16 A Cheese-Colored Camper

#17 Watch Your Whiskers, Stilton!

#18 Shipwreck on the Pirate Islands

#19 My Name Is Stilton, Geronimo Stilton

#20 Surf's Up, Geronimo!

#21 The Wild, Wild West

#22 The Secret of Cacklefur Castle

A Christmas Tale

#23 Valentine's Day Disaster

#24 Field Trip to Niagara Falls

#25 The Search for Sunken Treasure

#26 The Mummy with No Name

#27 The Christmas Toy Factory

#28 Wedding Crasher

#29 Down and Out Down Under

#30 The Mouse Island Marathon

#31 The Mysterious Cheese Thief

Christmas Catastrophe

#32 Valley of the Giant Skeletons

#33 Geronimo and the Gold Medal Mystery

#34 Geronimo Stilton, Secret Agent

#35 A Very Merry Christmas

#36 Geronimo's Valentine

#37 The Race Across America

#38 A Fabumouse School Adventure

#39 Singing Sensation

#40 The Karate Mouse

#41 Mighty Mount Kilimanjaro

#42 The Peculiar Pumpkin Thief

#43 I'm Not a Supermouse!

#44 The Giant Diamond Robbery

#45 Save the White Whale!

#46 The Haunted Castle

#47 Run for the Hills, Geronimo!

#48 The Mystery in Venice

#49 The Way of the Samurai

#50 This Hotel Is Haunted!

#51 The Enormouse Pearl Heist

#52 Mouse in Space!

#53 Rumble in the Jungle

Meet
GERONIMO STILTONOOT

He is a cavemouse — Geronimo Stilton's ancient ancestor! He runs the stone newspaper in the prehistoric village of Old Mouse City. From dealing with dinosaurs to dodging meteorites, his life in the Stone Age is full of adventure!

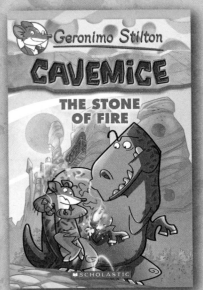

Geronimo Stilton

CAVEMICE

THE STONE OF FIRE

SCHOLASTIC

THE STONE OF FIRE

The Stone of Fire — the most precious artifact in the Old Mouse City mouseum — has been stolen! It's up to Geronimo Stiltonoot and his cavemouse friend Hercule Poirat to retrieve the stone from Tiger Khan and his band of fearsome felines.

Don't miss these very special editions!

   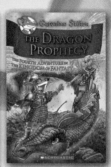

THE KINGDOM OF FANTASY

THE QUEST FOR PARADISE:
THE RETURN TO THE KINGDOM OF FANTASY

THE AMAZING VOYAGE:
THE THIRD ADVENTURE IN THE KINGDOM OF FANTASY

THE DRAGON PROPHECY:
THE FOURTH ADVENTURE IN THE KINGDOM OF FANTASY

Check out my first hardcover!

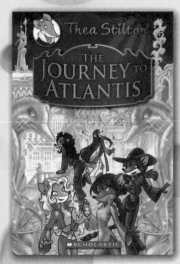

THEA STILTON:
THE JOURNEY TO ATLANTIS

THANKS FOR READING, AND GOOD-BYE UNTIL OUR NEXT ADVENTURE!

Thea Sisters